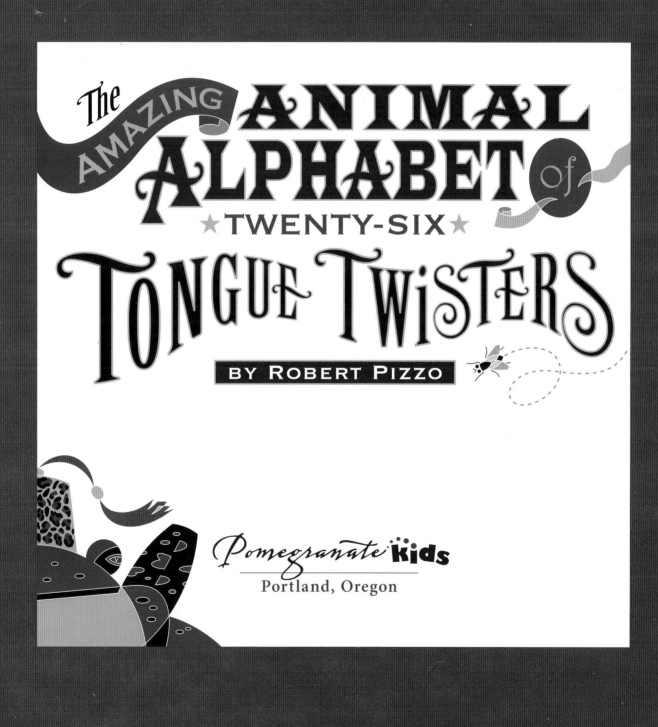

The Amazing ANIMAL ALPHABET of

★ TWENTY-SIX ★

Tongue Twisters

BY ROBERT PIZZO

Pomegranate **kids**

Portland, Oregon

For Gladys Graham and her Gaggle of Granddaughters

ig Brown Bull Blasts off a Badly Built Bright Blue Bicycle.

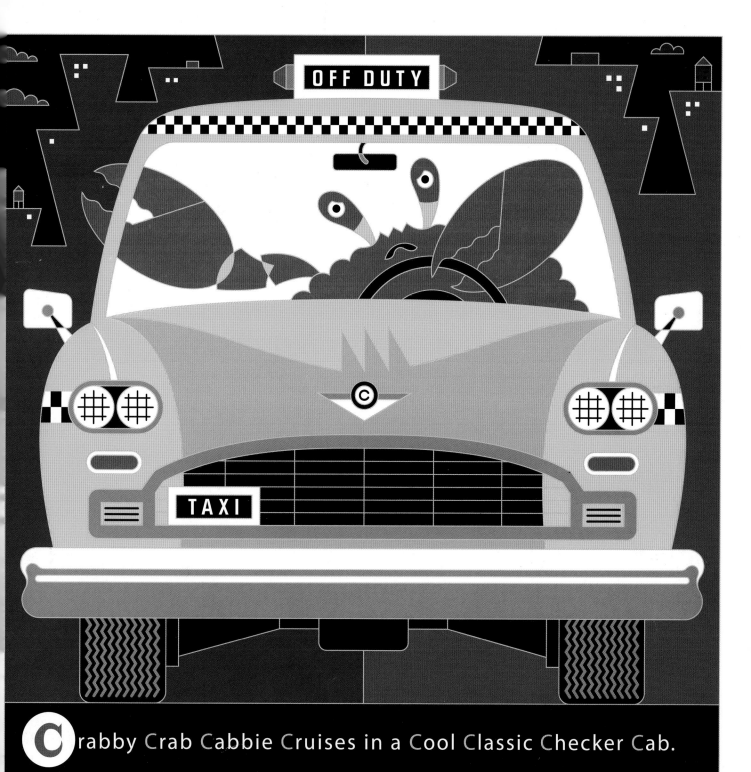

Crabby Crab Cabbie Cruises in a Cool Classic Checker Cab.

Delicate Dainty Dragonfly Darts from Daisies to Daffodils.

Enormously Elegant Elephant wears Electric Easter-Egg Earrings.

Fantastically Fearless Frog Flaunts a Funny Fake-Fur Fez.

Gigantic Gawky Gorilla Gets to Go in a Goofy Green Go-kart.

Hapless Hamsters Hurry Home on a Handcar in a Hailstorm.

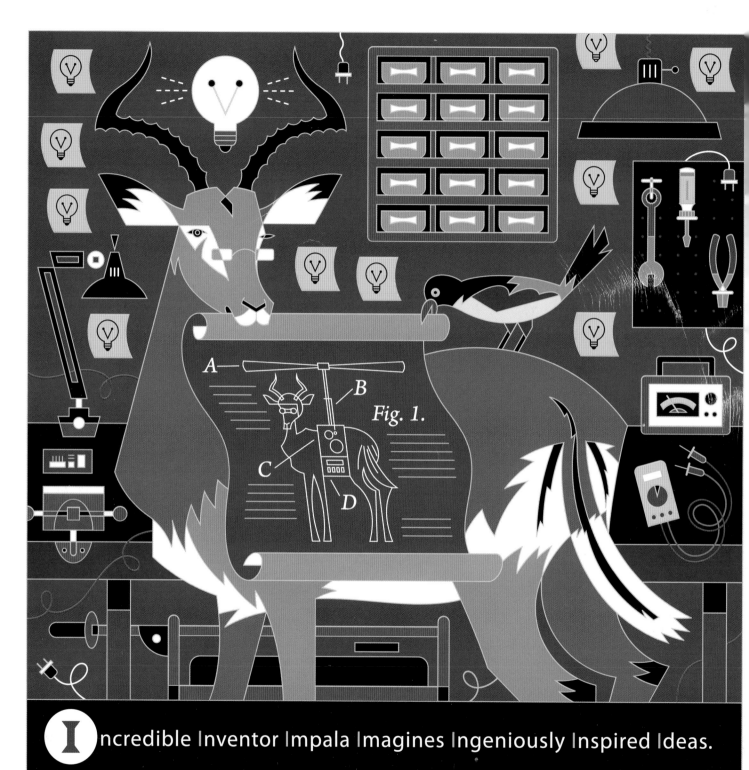

A

B

C

D

Fig. 1.

Incredible Inventor Impala Imagines Ingeniously Inspired Ideas.

Jaunty Jazzy Jackrabbit Jumps over a Junky Jalopy Jeep.

arate Kid Kangaroo Keeps Kicking a King-sized Knish Kabob.

Lazy Little Lion Lounges Leisurely on Lake Lucerne.

Mad Messy Monkeys Make too Much Macaroni on the Moon.

Natty Nightingale Neatly Nibbles Nachos in her Nest.

Outlandish ⊙ctopus ⊙rchestrates an ⊙boe ⊙rchestra of ⊙ne.

enguins Play Ping-Pong with Pretty Polka-dotted Paddles.

Quirky Queen bee Quietly Quilts a Quilt Quite nicely.

Rowdy Raunchy Red Rooster Really Rocks 'Round the clock.

Stinky Skunk in Smelly Sneakers Shows off on a Skateboard.

Techie Teenage Texan Tiger Texts Text To Tennessee Toads.

Uh, oh! Umbrellabird Utterly Underestimates Unearthly UFOs.

Vagabond Viper Vacations in a Valise in Vulture Valley.

Weak-Willed Waddling Weighty Walrus Waiter Wants Waffles.

X-ray fish goes eXploring on eXceptionally eXotic eXciting eXpeditions.

Y odeling Yammering Yachtsman Yak Yanks a Yolky Yellow Yo-Yo.

Zeppole-eating Zebra Zings on a Zippy Zany Zeppelin.

Published by PomegranateKids®, an imprint of
Pomegranate Communications, Inc.
19018 NE Portal Way, Portland OR 97230
800 227 1428 | www.pomegranate.com

Pomegranate Europe Ltd.
Unit 1, Heathcote Business Centre, Hurlbutt Road
Warwick, Warwickshire CV34 6TD, UK
[+44] 0 1926 430111 | sales@pomeurope.co.uk

To learn about new releases and special offers from Pomegranate, please visit www.pomegranate.com and sign up for
our e-mail newsletter. For all other queries, see "Contact Us" on our home page.

This product is in compliance with the Consumer Product Safety Improvement Act of 2008 (CPSIA). A General
Conformity Certificate concerning Pomegranate's compliance with the CPSIA is available on our website at
www.pomegranate.com, or by request at 800 227 1428.

Library of Congress Cataloging-in-Publication Data

Pizzo, Robert.
  The amazing animal alphabet : twenty-six tongue twisters / by Robert Pizzo.
    pages cm
  ISBN 978-0-7649-6622-4 (alk. paper)
  1. Alphabet--Juvenile literature. 2. Tongue twisters--Juvenile
    literature. 3. Riddles, Juvenile.   I. Title.
  PN6231.A45P59 2013
  428.1--dc23
                                2013005946
Pomegranate Catalog No. A224

Printed in China

22 21 20 19 18 17 16 15 14 13   10 9 8 7 6 5 4 3 2 1